T0198821

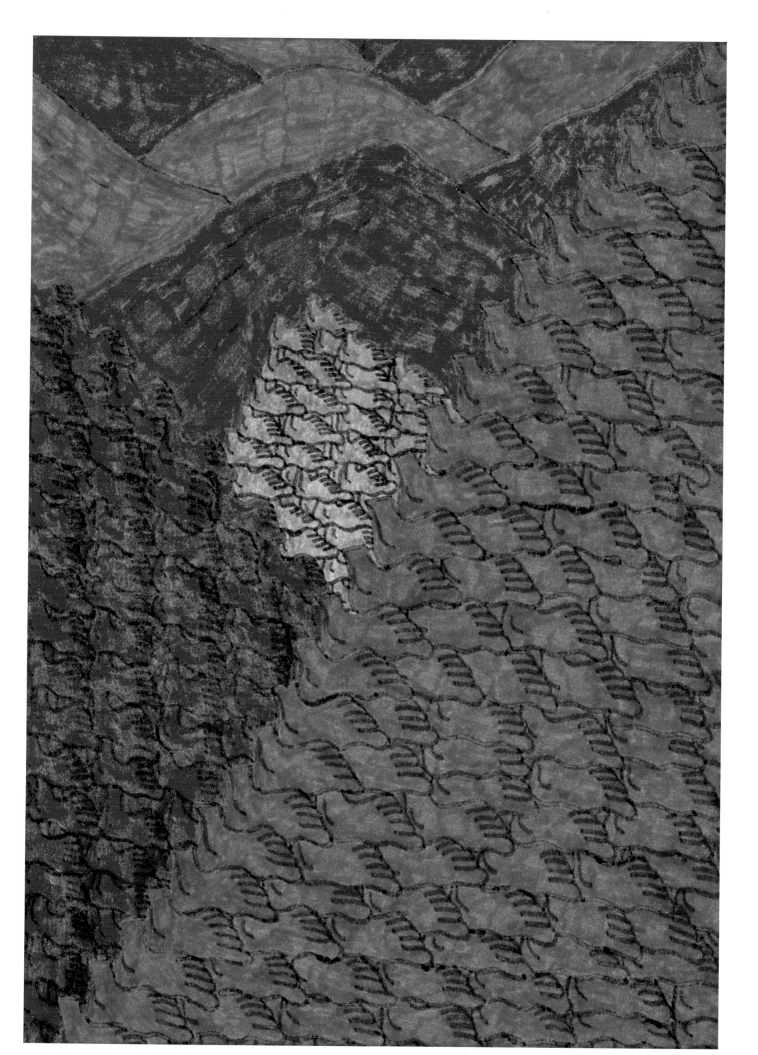

Sokhen

Among the boundless reaches of Queensridge,
Sokhen and Sokhit found a transfer.
Embracing the sacred object, it transported
them to Realmstone.

Sokhit

Grand Proliferator

Grazing the fertile pastures, both fallen Kings brought forth impurity, which quickly spread everywhere.

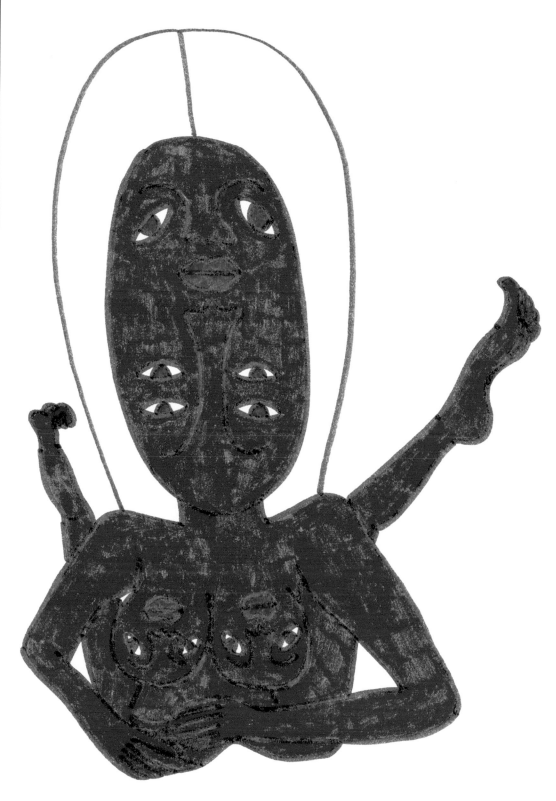

NeoKhmer Red Realmstone

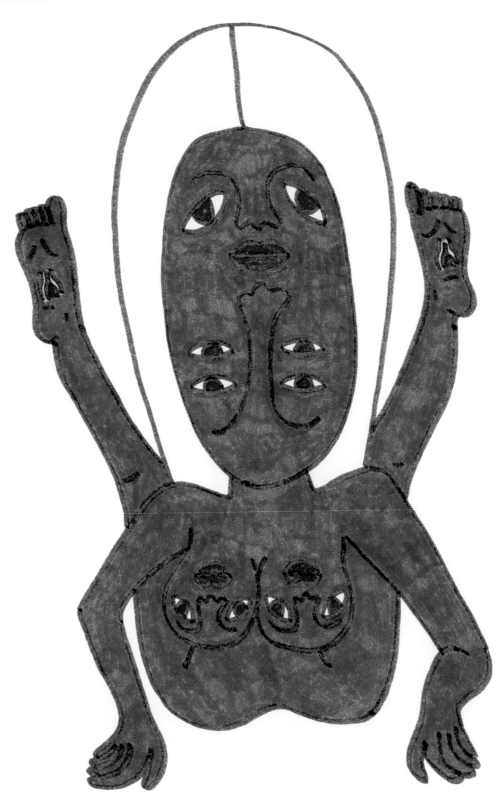

NeoKhmer Blue Realmstone

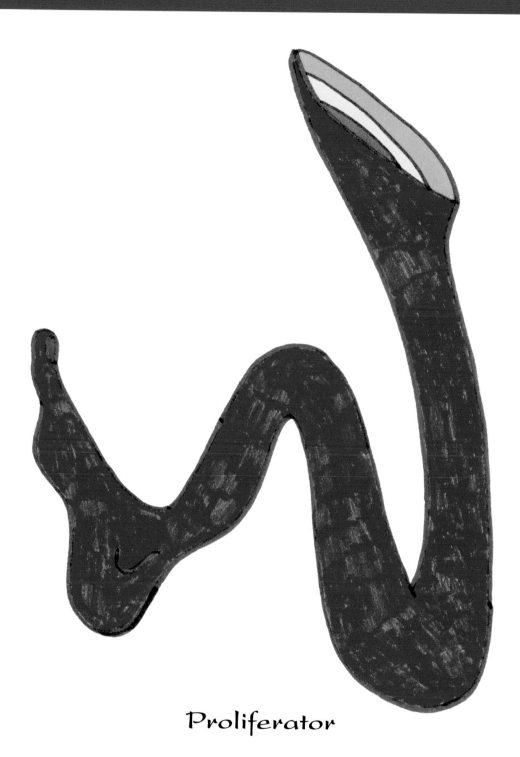

Proliferator

Kadao, Great Stewardess of Realmstone, saw the devastation and called upon the name of the Jade Princess Andevi.

Kadao

Interceding on her behalf, Andevi restored all back to its former glory. Relieved, Kadao thanked the Jade Princess.

Andevi

And Andevi sealed Sokhen and Sokhit inside
Kingsworth until the appointed time.

Order this book online at www.trafford.com
or email orders@trafford.com

Most Trafford titles are also available at major online book retailers.

 www.trafford.com

North America & international
toll-free: 844 688 6899 (USA & Canada)
fax: 812 355 4082

Our mission is to efficiently provide the world's finest, most
comprehensive book publishing service, enabling every author to
experience success. To find out how to publish your book, your way,
and have it available worldwide, visit us online at www.trafford.com

ISBN: 978-1-4251-2789-3 (e)

Print information available on the last page.

Trafford rev. 03/05/2021

Printed in the United States
by Baker & Taylor Publisher Services